PRAISE FOR MELODIE CAMPBELL'S
GODDAUGHTER SERIES

"Campbell's comic caper is just right for Jane Evanovich fans. Wacky family connections and snappy dialog make it impossible not to laugh."
—*Library Journal*

"The audience will enjoy the romance and... Campbell throws a few twists into the mix to add to the suspense."
—*CM Magazine*

"Campbell weaves a light, airy story with witty humor and a heroine with a likeable personality...Give this to readers who enjoy a deliciously funny tale."
—*VOYA*

"Another home run from Canada's funny girl, Melodie Campbell."
—*A Prairie Girl Reads* blog

"Strong plot, great zingers and imagery that draws you in and just doesn't let go."
—*Canadian Mystery Reviews*

WORST DATE EVER

MELODIE CAMPBELL

ORCA BOOK PUBLISHERS

Library and Archives Canada Cataloguing in Publication

Campbell, Melodie, 1955–, author
Worst date ever / Melodie Campbell.
(Rapid reads)

Issued in print and electronic formats.
ISBN 978-1-4598-1559-9 (softcover).—ISBN 978-1-4598-1560-5 (pdf).—
ISBN 978-1-4598-1561-2 (epub)

I. Title. II. Series: Rapid reads.
PS8605.A54745W67 2017   C813'.6   C2017-900807-2
C2017-900808-0

First published in the United States, 2017
Library of Congress Control Number: 2017932514

Summary: This funny short novel follows a single
mom on a number of first dates. (RL 3.1)

*Orca Book Publishers is dedicated to preserving the environment and has
printed this book on Forest Stewardship Council® certified paper.*

Orca Book Publishers gratefully acknowledges the support for
its publishing programs provided by the following agencies:
the Government of Canada through the Canada Book Fund and the
Canada Council for the Arts, and the Province of British Columbia
through the BC Arts Council and the Book Publishing Tax Credit.

Cover design by Jenn Playford
Cover photography by Getty Images and iStock.com

ORCA BOOK PUBLISHERS
www.orcabook.com

Printed and bound in Canada.

20 19 18 17 • 4 3 2 1

For my friends at the
Hamilton Literacy Council

ONE

One day I am going to write a book. It is going to be called *A Dummy's Guide to Men*. It will include all sorts of useful tips, such as how to find Prince Charming in a sea of Prince Ronalds.

I am well qualified to write about this subject. This is because I have recently met a lot of Prince Ronalds. I met them all through an online dating site. I blame my friend Angela for pushing me into online dating. She also gave me the idea for the book. It started like this...

"You signed up?" said Angela. She plunked down onto the plastic chair opposite me.

I nodded. "Yup. E-Galaxy, here I come."

"It's time." Angela cradled her coffee mug with both hands. "It's been two years, Jennie. Two years since Greg died. It's time you started dating."

She could say his name now without me bursting into tears. So I guess time had done some healing. But it had been such a shock. Who expects their husband to die of a heart attack at thirty-four?

I forced the thought from my mind and instead filled my mouth with coffee.

It was Sunday evening. We were seated in the Original Coffeehouse, a cute little coffee bistro on Main. It was close to my new apartment. Angela said they had the best coffee in town. Better than the chains.

It was cheap and cheerful. Not dark and expensive like some of the uptown bistros that aped New York. I felt comfortable here, enveloped in the aroma of freshly brewed, rich coffee. Is there any better smell in the world?

"You need to get back on the horse," said Angela, pointing a perfectly manicured finger at me.

"Don't be a nag," I quipped, putting my mug down.

Angela was my best friend. I'd known her since high school. She and Zack had met each other three years ago. Now she was happily married and wanted everyone else to be. That's the sort of nice person she was. But she could also be kind of pushy.

"You have to tell me every detail," she ordered. "Of every date you go on."

"Of course I will!" I said. No I won't, I thought.

Angela is a great pal, but she works as a hair stylist. I know better than to tell her all the gory details. That hair salon thrives on gossip.

Of course, Angela always looks fabulous. Perfect hair, dyed a fashionable blond, with a great cut.

My hair is pretty ordinary, long and chocolate brown. I can't complain, because Angela gives me a great deal on cuts. And I like my natural hair color. It matches my eyes.

We are different in other ways too. Angela is outgoing. I'm more quiet. Angela is like glamorous Ginger on *Gilligan's Island*. I'm a Mary Ann.

"Let's call this Operation Prince Charming. I like that," she said, obviously pleased with herself. "Operation PC for short, in case anyone is listening in."

I grinned back at her. "Cute. Sort of like we're on a secret mission."

"You've taken the next two weeks off?" Angela pushed a stray lock of golden hair behind her ear.

"Yes." I work as a customer-service rep in a bank. "I'm on vacation. Ryan is in school. I thought it would be better to blitz this. Meet as many men as possible in two weeks."

She nodded her approval. "That's smart. Meet them during the day, and not after dark. But I bet it's more than that." She skewered me with her look. "You want to do this before your parents come back from Florida, right?"

I laughed at that. "Guilty as charged." It was early April. Mom and Dad own a trailer in Florida. Dad has retired from his job at the steel plant and has bad arthritis. They winter in Orlando now to avoid the cold. They would be back by May 1.

My parents had been wonderful when Greg died. They were great with Ryan.

But you didn't want your parents looking over your shoulder when you were dating.

"You'll need to take off your wedding ring," she said.

I looked quickly down at my hand. "I will. Tonight."

A man in a barista apron appeared at Angela's shoulder. "Long time no see. How are you doing, Angela?"

"Dave!" She gave him a big smile. Then she turned to me. "Jennie, Dave owns this place. You should get to know him."

Dave raised an eyebrow. I blushed fiercely.

"What I mean is," Angela continued, "Jennie's a widow. She just joined E-Galaxy. I've told her she should meet her dates here, where it's safe."

"Angela, shhh! You're embarrassing me," I said.

"Why?" She looked surprised.

"No need to be embarrassed about trying to find someone to share your life with," Dave said. He had a nice low voice. And then, more quietly, he added, "I'm sorry about your husband."

That was a kind thing to say. I took a longer look at him. Dave was of medium height, with dark-brown hair. His face was pleasant but not what you would call handsome. Too angular to be cute. Just an ordinary guy.

"You'll look out for her, right?" my friend said. "Some of these guys might be creepy."

"ANG!" I scolded.

"Sure thing." He gave me a big smile. "I'm here most of the time. Just signal if you want me. Now I'd better get back to the counter." He saluted like a soldier, then turned and walked away.

"What a nice guy," I said, watching him leave.

"Yeah," said Angela. "Too bad he's married."

Of course he was. I finished the rest of my coffee.

"So back to E-Galaxy. Have you seen their cool ad on television?"

I nodded. *"E-Galaxy—Our Matches Are Out of This World!"*

"Don't knock it," said Angela. "My cousin Tara met her husband on E-Galaxy. He's a great guy. They got married last spring in Vegas."

I smiled over my coffee mug. "I'm just poking fun at the concept. They call it E-Galaxy. Like you have the whole galaxy to choose from, not just earth."

"Haven't you heard, Jennie? Men are from Mars." Angela always made me smile.

"I hope they're not all on Mars," I said.

TWO

I logged in to E-Galaxy as soon as I got home. Operation Prince Charming was off to a brilliant start. The E-Galaxy program had matched me with over two dozen men in my age group. At least eight had commented on my profile already. Six had asked if they could meet me that week. You had the choice of emailing back and forth first. I phoned Angela to ask her advice.

"Meet them in person," she said. "You don't want to get attached to anyone by email and then find out they are losers in person."

Losers in person? I wasn't sure what she meant by that. But I followed her advice anyway.

On Monday evening I decided to come clean with my son, Ryan.

"What would you think if I started dating?" I said to him. We were having a quick dinner of hot dogs in the kitchen before homework time.

He was silent for a few moments, munching the last few bites. Then he looked up at me with Greg's eyes.

"I think Dad would say it was about time," he said solemnly.

Sometimes Ryan took my breath away. It wasn't only the way he resembled his father. Ryan had a maturity that was way beyond his age. Grief will do that.

"But what do *you* think?" I asked.

He picked up a paper napkin and wiped his mouth. "Mom, I'm nearly thirteen. You can't expect me to be around forever.

I can't keep you company when you're old. Of course you need someone."

His cell phone buzzed from over on the kitchen counter. We had a strict rule about no cell phones during meals. Ryan looked up at me hopefully.

"Go," I said, waving a hand.

He launched himself from the table and snatched up the phone.

I sat back and looked around the cozy kitchen in the apartment that had become our new home. It was a nice bright unit, in a good neighborhood close to Ryan's school. We each had our own bedroom. We were comfortable here. But it wasn't the house we had shared with his father. I had sold that when it became clear that my modest salary wouldn't cover the mortgage.

No, Ryan wouldn't be here forever. He was hardly here even now. My heart swelled, thinking about what a good kid he was. Greg would have been proud of him.

"Just watch out for creeps."

"What?" I said, coming out of my thoughts.

"There are a lot of creeps out there," said Ryan, still staring down at the phone. "You're pretty innocent, Mom."

"*What?*" I said again. My twelve-year-old son was calling me innocent?

"You and Dad got married young. You don't know what it's like out there," said Ryan. He pocketed his cell phone. I watched his lanky form disappear into his bedroom.

Jeans are getting short, I thought. He's growing again.

I logged in to E-Galaxy while Ryan did his homework. I did a lot of responding to prospective dates. Two more men had expressed interest in meeting me. I looked at the eight available and chose six. It was surprisingly easy to eliminate two. Or at least to postpone meeting them.

For instance, Daniel. Daniel said his hobbies were guns and hunting. I was puzzled that we had been matched at all. I wasn't into either of those things. But then I noticed he'd said he liked kids and dogs. I had mentioned that on my profile too. He was the right age. So maybe that had been enough to match us.

The other match I decided not to act on immediately was Timmy. First of all, I had a problem with a grown-up man who would call himself Timmy. It made me suspicious that his mother still did his laundry. On his profile, he said that his hobby was model trains. It appeared to be his only hobby. I had nothing against model trains. But I hoped to find someone who had interests that intrigued me.

So I ended the E-Galaxy session with six coffee dates lined up. That was a lot of dates for one week. Surely at least one of them would be a nice guy.

Later that night, in the privacy of my bedroom, I took off my wedding ring.

I'd done it before, once, a few months back. Experimenting. It felt weird. Hard to explain why. It's sort of like when you take off your clothes at night and you can feel your nakedness. Your skin is cold. You need a blanket around you to feel secure.

My finger felt cold.

Would I ever feel secure again?

THREE

The next morning I was looking forward to my first coffee date. It's fair to say I was pretty excited. And nervous.

I liked the sound of Phil from his online profile. He had three children. He worked for a software firm. He really loved animals. His profile photo showed a man with medium-brown hair and light eyes. He had a short beard and a nice, friendly smile. Not bad looking, although I wasn't crazy about beards. His clothes though! Angela would have a fit about his clothes. They might have been fashionable in the '90s. I had to smile, because the photo said it all. Phil was a nerd. In some ways, this was good. He obviously didn't have a woman looking after him.

So I decided he would be good first-date material. You could always do something about clothes if things worked out, I reasoned.

Thinking of clothes, I had to come up with an outfit for myself. What should one wear on a blind date at a coffee bar? Nothing too sexy, I decided. Not that I had much in that department.

I stood in front of my closet for a long time. The problem was, I didn't have any date clothes. In fact, I hadn't bought anything new in two years. Money had been tight after Greg died.

We hadn't had much equity in the house. Most of it had been eaten up by lawyer and real estate fees. A small insurance policy had paid for Greg's funeral. I'd paid off the car loan and our credit-card debt with the rest of the money. I even tore up the credit cards so I couldn't accumulate any more debt.

Ryan and I managed to live on my bank-teller salary alone, but it didn't allow for a lot of extravagances.

Back to the closet. Maybe the black tulip skirt would do. It came to just above my knees. I liked the way it swirled when I walked.

Angela had recommended that I wear a bright color on top so I could tell my date how to find me. I had two bright knit tops. One was red, the other pink. Greg had loved me in red. He said it looked great with my dark hair. I remembered him liking the song "Lady in Red" and singing along. For a moment the sadness started to creep back. Don't go there, I ordered myself.

I decided on the other top. Pink was good. It had a flattering scooped neck, but not too low. I could be the lady in pink.

➤ ➤ ➤

At ten minutes to two I arrived at the Original Coffeehouse.

Dave was there, working alongside a teenage girl behind the counter who was busy making blended drinks. He took my order and then brought my café mocha over to the table.

"You look nice. I like the pink. Big date today?" he said.

I met his eyes and grinned. "My first."

"Nervous?"

"A little." I breathed in the luscious coffee fumes. "Gee, it smells good in here."

"We aim to please," he said. Then he chuckled. "Think I'm addicted to the smell of this place. My blood must be half java by now." He waved as he walked to the back.

The bell on the coffee-shop door dingled. An older man with thinning gray hair and a beard walked in. I looked back down at my cell phone.

Two texts from Angela, demanding to know if it had "happened yet."

Another text from Ryan, asking if he could stay at a friend's house for dinner.

"Jennie?"

I looked up. It was the same older man. He had to be well over fifty. He couldn't be my date!

The man sat down. "You look just like your photo."

But you don't look anything like yours!

"Phil?" I squeaked.

"What's the matter? Am I late?"

By about twenty years.

"Sorry." I gulped, trying to recover my composure. "I didn't recognize you from your profile picture."

"I've always loved that photo. I look great in that one."

Yes, but about two decades younger, I wanted to scream. No wonder the clothes had seemed retro!

"You said you were thirty-eight," I said. My eyes seemed to be transfixed on the bald patch at the front of his head.

He smiled with yellowed teeth. "Oh, everyone fibs a little on those profiles. No harm done."

No harm done? The man had lied! Didn't they check these things at E-Galaxy?

"I have a twelve-year-old son," I blurted out.

"That's okay. I love kids. Here, let me show you pictures of my grandchildren."

He pulled out a wallet and started unraveling a plastic accordion of photos.

"This is Sarah. She's eight. These are the twins, Matty and Mark…" He continued to flip pictures and point to additional children. I zoned out to the drone of his voice.

How could this be happening? My first date in fifteen years, and it had been hijacked by Father Time.

Angela had told me not to be afraid to cut the date short if it wasn't turning out well. I took a minute to gather my courage. Then I came right out with it.

"Look, Phil. I can see you're a very nice person. But I don't think this is going to work out. I have a young son to raise. I'm really looking for someone my own age."

Phil looked up from his photos. The wrinkles on his face sagged for a moment. But only a moment.

"That's okay," he said with a voice full of bravado. "I really only date blondes. I only made an exception this time because you were pretty."

21

I was still sitting there with my mouth open when he walked out the door.

Dave came over almost immediately.

"A little old for you?" he said.

"He has seven grandchildren!" I said, waving my arms around.

Dave laughed. "Well, if it's any consolation, he seemed really into you."

I threw my napkin at him. That only made him laugh harder.

FOUR

The next day I looked forward to meeting my second candidate.

But first I called Angela to tell her about the night before.

"He was a Prince Ronald!" I wailed.

"I'm not exactly sure what you mean by that," said Angela.

Then I remembered. She didn't have kids. So she wouldn't be familiar with a book called *The Paper Bag Princess*. In it, Prince Ronald is a dweeb. He looks good on paper, but he turns out to be a bum. The princess ends up saving the day.

I explained this to Angela. She laughed out loud.

"So the score is one Prince Ronald and no Prince Charmings. Hopefully, your date today will be better."

"If he's under forty and breathing, it will be better," I said to her. We clicked off.

I had arranged to meet Owen at two in the afternoon. He said he drove a truck. I assumed that's why he could get time off to meet during the workday.

Owen had those blond good looks that you associate with Nordic people. He looked a lot like a guy I dated briefly in high school. That fellow had been sweet, but his family moved away after eleventh grade. I was sad, of course. But I met Greg soon after, and my life took a different turn.

Don't think about Greg, I reminded myself.

According to his profile, Owen loved being outdoors. He enjoyed animal documentaries on television and fishing.

I wasn't much into fishing. But I did love animals and being outdoors.

Maybe this one wouldn't be a loser. After all, he looked like Prince Charming.

I got to the Original Coffeehouse about one forty-five. I wanted to arrive there early so I could get my café mocha and settle in at the same table as on the day before. It gave me a sense of security, being there first.

There was only one other couple in the shop. They were each reading a section of the newspaper. Long-marrieds, now retired, I deduced. Comfortable in each other's company. I envied them.

Dave greeted me with a grin and a twinkle in his eye. "Heard from Grandpa?" he said.

"Don't," I said. "Don't even start." I waggled my finger at him, and he chuckled.

The Original Coffeehouse had a bright sixties vibe, but the beverage equipment was all up to date. I watched him prepare the café mocha using a sleek black-and-steel Italian espresso maker. His movements were swift but careful. I breathed in the wonderful aroma of freshly ground beans.

"So Angela tells me you're writing a book," he said.

"What?" Angela said that? I only meant it as a joke!

"Does it have anything to do with this E-Galaxy experiment you have going on here?" He handed me the café mocha.

I took the mug and cleared my throat. "Sort of," I said, thinking fast. "But it's supposed to be a secret." Since I didn't know I was really writing it, it was a very good secret indeed.

"Won't tell—Scout's honor," he said.

I walked swiftly back to my usual table. My face was burning.

Now Dave thought I was writing a book! What would he think if I told him the working title? *A Dummy's Guide to Men* might make him laugh. Or it might not. He might be insulted. Or embarrassed.

Dave was a nice guy, and I liked him. I wouldn't want to take that chance.

While I was musing about this, the clock on the wall moved past two. I checked my cell phone for any new messages. Nothing.

I surfed the Net for the next while.

When I looked up again it was ten minutes past two. Still no date.

Prince Charming was swiftly turning into Prince Ronald.

I'd stay until two thirty, I told myself.

At two twenty-five, a tall blond guy sauntered into the shop. He looked dazed.

Actually, it might be more accurate to say he looked daft.

He spotted me and came over.

"Pink," he said.

Good thing I'd worn the top. "Hi," I said brightly. "I'm Jennie."

"Sorry I'm late," he said. "My truck broke down. I had to take the bus."

So that's why he was late! Now I felt better.

He stood with his hands in his jean-jacket pockets, gazing off into space. "Do you happen to have any change for a coffee? I used up everything I had for the bus."

Now I felt worse.

"Uh, sure," I said. I reached into my purse and pulled out four dollars.

"And a donut? I haven't eaten all day."

I pulled out another dollar.

He went up to the counter and gave his order. My cell phone buzzed. I looked down at it. **Is this one Prince Charming?** texted Angela.

Ronald, I texted back.

Owen came back to the table with a large coffee and two donuts. He didn't give one to me.

"Did you have any cargo on your truck?" I said. I wondered if the goods were perishable. That could be awful. I once heard about a truckload of chickens that were stuck in an overturned truck for hours, poor things.

"Huh?" He didn't look up from the donut he was wolfing down.

"I wondered if you were carrying perishable cargo on the truck."

He looked up from the donut at last. But it didn't help. He was clearly baffled.

"You said your truck broke down." I enunciated the words carefully, as if to a small child. "Were you in the middle of a job?"

Still no signs of life in his eyes.

"You're a trucker, right?" I was starting to wonder if I had it wrong. This was the guy who drove a truck, wasn't it? Had I gotten things mixed up?

"Oh," he said, finally catching on. "It's an old pickup truck. I got it real cheap from my uncle Ed at the junkyard."

He stuffed the last half of the second donut into his mouth.

"Jennie, can you come here a minute?" Dave called from the behind the counter.

Relief flooded over me. "I'll just be a second," I said to the nontrucker.

I made it to the counter in record time. Dave waved an arm for me to join him around the back.

"That guy is so stoned he can't even walk straight. Get rid of him, Jennie."

The light dawned. "Is that what it is?" I said, looking back to the table. Nontrucker was now looking under the table for used gum. He found some and popped it into his mouth.

I shivered and grabbed Dave's arm.

"Help me," I pleaded.

He snorted. "Sure thing."

Dave walked right up to my date and tapped him on the shoulder. "Sorry, man. We're closing." Dave grabbed him gently by the arm and guided him upright.

Owen started to walk toward the door. Then he stopped. Hesitated. He turned back to Dave and said, "Do you have a couple of bucks for the bus?"

FIVE

Later that night I phoned Angela. Honestly, I was becoming her nightly entertainment.

"Oh no. *No*. No one is that rude, crude and socially unacceptable," she said. And then she hooted in laughter. "And borrowing money from you. On a first date!"

"Not only that, but it was the first thing out of his mouth," I said. "I think that officially qualifies him as a loser."

"Prince Ronald, in the flesh," she said. "Well, at least it's a good one for the book."

That book again. Maybe I would have to write it.

"So you've met Old Guy, and Stoned Guy," said Angela.

"Pretty good for only two dates, eh?" I said.

"This is better than the comedy club. But really, Jennie. Did it never occur to you that if they can meet during the day, they probably don't have jobs?" said Angela.

"I'm starting to catch on," I said.

And I was. I made sure the next date was gainfully employed.

In his E-Galaxy profile, Scott said he was a financial analyst with an investment firm. I recognized the name of the company from ads in the newspaper. But men could say a lot of things that weren't true, I was finding out.

So I did something a teeny bit sketchy. I looked him up on the Internet.

Even now, I'm not proud of this. It sounds too much like stalking, and I hadn't even met the guy yet. But it did pay off. I went to the investment firm's website. I located the search function and typed in *Scott*. Yup, a Scott popped up. His photo was even the same as the one on the E-Galaxy site. So his age listed there was probably legitimate too.

What a relief! At least he seemed to be who he said he was.

I stared at the photo for some time. He looked a little bit like Greg. Light-brown hair cut short. Narrow face. Wire-rim glasses. Serious expression. He was wearing a dark-blue business suit. This was a business photo, I reminded myself. Scott would be hoping to attract business clients with this picture.

I went back to the E-Galaxy profile. Never married and no kids. Scott liked fine dining and going to the theater. I could get used to fine dining. It would be fun to see something in a theater besides superhero movies.

So I agreed to meet him for coffee after work on Thursday. Once again, I wore my black tulip skirt and pretty pink top.

There were probably a dozen people in the Original Coffeehouse when I arrived. All of them were looking down at their cell phones. Dave came to the counter when he saw me waiting.

"Are these people capable of talking?" I gestured around. "Or do they only communicate with their fingers?"

Dave chuckled. I liked his low voice. "It is rather quiet in here today. Not that I mind. It's when they all talk on their cell phones that I get annoyed."

I looked around the place while waiting for my coffee. The Original Coffeehouse indeed looked original. The predominant color was teal, with beige accents. I loved it.

Light poured in from the huge picture windows at the front and side.

When my coffee was ready, I took my place at the usual table. I took out my cell phone.

Angela had left me a text. **Boring at work. Let me know how it goes.**

"Jennie?"

I looked up. The guy in front of me was the sort of man who would impress my parents. His gray business suit was neatly pressed. He was wearing a subtle tie. His shirt had French cuffs. His hair was clipped short. But his expression was oh so serious. If anything, he was even more businesslike in person than he'd looked in his photo. I wondered if the photographer had done something to make Scott smile in that picture. I had visions of the photographer holding up a rubber ducky and squeaking it.

I covered my giggle with a smile. "Hi, Scott, nice to meet you."

"Your directions were impeccable." Scott sat down. "I also appreciate that you informed me about the pink top. Very efficient."

Well. That was something you didn't hear every day from a date.

"Would you like a coffee?" I asked.

Scott shook his head. "I don't drink coffee. No caffeine for me. Herbal tea, if they have it."

That was weird. I could almost hear Angela say, *Do you really want to date a guy who doesn't drink coffee?*

I waited for Scott to get up from the table to give his order at the counter. But he didn't move.

Then I wondered if he expected me to get it for him. But it wasn't that.

Scott stared across the table at me. His eyes were concentrating fiercely. You know how people who collect butterflies pin them to boards? That's what I felt like. One of those butterflies.

He must have approved, because then he smiled for the first time. A thin, satisfied smile. No teeth showing.

"Let's get right to it then, shall we?" he said. I watched as he pulled a sheet of paper from the inside pocket of his jacket. He carefully unfolded it. Then he took out a pen.

He read from the sheet in front of him. "The company may decide to move me to New York. Would you be willing to move to another city with me?" His eyes lifted to meet mine.

I gulped. "Is that a checklist?"

"Yes," he said apologetically. "I know. How embarrassing to use paper. But Mom doesn't trust computers."

Mom? His mom wrote a checklist?

"Would you mind standing up?" he asked.

I stood up without thinking.

"Child-bearing hips. Good." He made a tick mark on the paper. "I know you have one son. I assume you wouldn't mind having another child or two? You're young enough, right?" He scanned the paper. "Thirty-four, it says here. That's fine, if we hurry."

Hurry?

"Do you go to church?"

"What?" I squeaked. I wasn't over the last shock yet.

He shook his head. "Let's skip that one. I don't really care one way or the other. Mom wrote that question."

"Dave?" I cried out in an unusually high voice.

He was over to our table in five seconds flat.

"Everything okay, sis?" said Dave. He frowned at my date.

"This man is your brother?" said Scott. He lifted his head and pushed his glasses farther up the bridge of his nose. "That's excellent. I have all sorts of questions about the family here. Just give me a second..." He looked back down at the sheet of paper and flipped it over.

"I don't think so," said Dave. He crossed his arms against his chest. "We're a pretty private family. Connected, if you get my drift. You don't want to mess with us."

"Connected? As in..." Scott's voice drifted off.

"Yes," said Dave. "And I think it would be safer for you if you left right now."

"Safer," repeated Scott. He pushed his glasses higher again. "Yes." He sprang up from the table and walked out the door. He didn't even say goodbye.

I started to giggle then. Dave sat down across from me. He smiled when he saw me laughing.

"Brother? You're my brother?" I said.

"Worked, didn't it?" He relaxed back into the chair. "We might want to use that again."

"I always wanted an older brother," I said wistfully.

"Who says I'm older?" said Dave. His eyes twinkled at me.

I took a better look at him. We could be related, I supposed. We both had dark-brown hair and brown eyes. My eyes dropped to his shoulders. He had wide shoulders and muscular arms, just like the men in my family. I'd noticed that a few minutes earlier, when he crossed his arms.

"What's wrong?" said Dave. His eyebrows had scrunched into a frown.

I shook myself sternly. "Nothing," I said. "I was just thinking how nice it would be to have a brother."

"Are you an only child?"

I nodded. "You?"

"Nope. Three brothers. I'm the youngest."

"Wow," I said. "That must be wonderful."

He snorted. "Not always. I learned how to fight at an early age."

He paused. The silence got a bit awkward. Then he said, "Are you back here tomorrow?"

I nodded. "I'm on a schedule. I only have another week."

"What do you mean?"

"Another week off work," I said. "I only have two weeks to complete this project. Then my parents get back from Florida."

He chuckled. "So they don't know you're doing this."

"Heck no," I said. I fought off an urge to shiver. "But my son does. I wouldn't hide it from him."

"That's smart," said Dave. He paused. "What are you doing tonight? More dates?"

"I have to go to Ryan's school. Sign-up for soccer." I glanced down at my cell phone to check the time. "I should probably be going."

"See you tomorrow," Dave said. We both stood up.

"Bye." I waved as I walked out the door.

SIX

As soon as I got in the door, Ryan surprised me.

"Mom, I want to see where you're meeting these guys," he said.

I had to smile. Bad enough having to worry about my parents interfering. Now I had my son looking over my shoulder.

"It's perfectly safe," I said. "It's at a coffee shop. The owner is a friend of Angela's."

"Take me there," he said. "That way I'll know where you are."

I raised an eyebrow.

"You always want to know where I am," he said.

Oh brother. My own words coming back to haunt me. How could you argue with logic like that? Practice what you preach, I told myself.

"Fair enough," I said. "We'll go there on Saturday morning."

At ten to seven, it was time for soccer sign-up at Ryan's school. We got into the car. "You could just drop me off," Ryan said.

"I can't. I'm pretty sure we have to give them a check tonight. They may not hold your place unless you pay in advance."

"You could write the check and just drop me off."

"We don't know the total amount. There might be taxes," I said.

I could almost hear the wheels churning in his mind.

"You could give me a blank check, and I could write in the amount myself."

I raised my eyebrow. "Not doing that. It's not legal."

He moaned. He was getting good at that, practicing to be a teenager.

I knew what was going on, of course. He didn't want to be seen with his mother in front of the other kids.

"Look. You can go into the gym and get the paperwork," I said. "Bring it back to me in the hall, and I'll write the check. Then you can hand it in yourself."

We settled on that.

"I don't know why you're so embarrassed to be with me," I said, looking in the rearview mirror. "Everyone has a mother."

"You just wouldn't understand," he mumbled.

That was another thing he was getting good at. Mumbling.

But I did understand, actually. It came down to one word. *Girls*.

In the last few months Ryan had discovered girls. I didn't know it specifically. Meaning, I hadn't actually heard him say it. But it was in his actions.

Very suddenly he was taking more care with his appearance. He wouldn't wear clothes that appeared childish or dirty. He spent more than a few minutes in the bathroom in the morning. And he was getting fussy about his hair.

These were the worst times—the times when I really missed Greg. Ryan needed a man in his life. My dad was great, but he was old. No teenage boy wants advice on how to be popular with girls from his grandpa.

I pulled my trusty Ford into a parking spot close to the exit. Ryan was out of the car in a flash. I didn't bother to catch up with him. He would find me in the hall.

The place was a madhouse. The second I walked into the foyer, I wished

I'd brought ear muffs. Everyone was using their "outdoor voices." Kids were running to and fro, excited to greet one another. Which always made me smile, as they had seen each other all day at school.

I walked down the main hall toward the gym. Ryan was already out of sight.

A small group of women had gathered just down from the gymnasium entrance. I recognized one of them from my own high school days. She and Angela still kept in touch. We saw each other from time to time at school events now. Debbie called from across the sea of young kids scooting back and forth. She smiled a welcome as I walked over to join them.

"Banished to the hall?" I said to her.

She laughed. "You know how boys are at this age."

Debbie introduced me to the two other women she was standing with. I had seen both of them before. They were mothers of kids in the same grade as Ryan.

"So Ang tells me you're trying E-Galaxy," said Debbie.

Darn that Angela! Who else did she tell?

"You remember Sandy Walker from eleventh grade? She met a great guy online. They're married now," Debbie said.

"How wonderful," I said, sighing inwardly. Sandy probably took the last Prince Charming, leaving me with all the Ronalds.

"I know this woman who met a guy on E-Galaxy. He seemed really nice," said the woman with short red hair. Her name was Lindsay.

It seemed everyone had a story about online dating. Were all women but me destined to meet a nice guy on E-Galaxy?

"Then he moved in with her and ran off with all her money," Lindsay finished.

"Total scumbag!" said Debbie.

"Was his name Owen?" I said under my breath.

"That's even worse than Meat Guy," said the blonde called Christine.

Meat Guy?

"Josie Harmon went out to dinner with a guy she met online. She's a vegetarian. When he found out, he couldn't stop talking about meat. Apparently, he really likes meat. All kinds. He talked about the different cuts of beef, where they came from. In detail." The woman shook her head.

"That sounds awful!" said Debbie.

"Sure was. She didn't make it…" Her cell phone buzzed. Her voice trailed off as she looked down at it, distracted.

"Through the date?" I asked.

"To the bathroom. She threw up all over the spaghetti."

Ryan came charging through the double doors. "All done, Mom. I'm signed up. We can pay on the first day."

"He's looking tall," Debbie said to me.

"Don't say a word," I said back to her. "Mothers are supposed to be seen and not heard."

Christine laughed. "They aren't supposed to exist at all."

SEVEN

*T*hursday was day four of Project PC. I had a coffee date with Garry Reimer on Friday at four o'clock. Usually we aren't given the last names of people on the dating site. This is for security reasons, I was told. Internet scamming is a big threat these days. Scammers can gather a lot of information about you from these sites if they know your full name.

But Garry hadn't worried about that. He'd told me his last name right off. This was because he is a real estate agent. More on that later.

At three forty-five I pulled my old Ford Focus into the second-to-last vacant parking spot at the Original Coffeehouse. This was a busy time of day. I wondered if Garry would have to park on the street.

That delicious aroma of rich coffee hit me as soon as I entered the shop. I stopped just inside the door to savor it for a moment. Funny how specific odors can make you feel so good. My instinct was to close my eyes. Maybe we can smell better if our eyes are closed.

Dave was occupied doing something behind the counter, as usual. The same teenage girl from before was at the cash. She had long honey-blond hair and a warm smile. When she saw me, she turned and said, "Dave. Your friend is here."

Dave looked up and gave me a crooked grin. "I put a Reserved sign on your table."

"You did?" I looked back to the seating area. There it was. A tent card with *Reserved* printed on it. Had it been there all day? Had I told Dave what time I'd be in? I didn't think so.

"Thanks!" I said.

Dave nodded. He still had his hands full.

"Café mocha?" the young girl said. The name tag on her shirt said *Caitlin*.

"Yes. Thanks, Caitlin."

I sat down at the table and reviewed what I remembered about Garry.

He was a year younger than me. That didn't happen often. Most men on E-Galaxy were after younger women, it seemed. Much younger, in many cases. My first Prince Ronald had been a prime example. (More accurately, a "past his prime" example.)

My date today was way different.

Garry had never been married. He didn't have kids. His interests were golfing (ick) and reading nonfiction, especially magazines.

I would have preferred it to be fiction, because that's what I like to read. But at least it showed he was literate. We would have things to talk about.

Dave delivered my café mocha personally. "Who's it today? What number? I've lost count."

I frowned at him while still smiling. Funny how it is possible to do both at the same time. "Number five. He's a real estate agent."

"Uh-oh," said Dave. His eyes twinkled at me.

"What do you mean, *uh-oh*?" I said.

He shook his head and gave me the usual shrug. "You'll see." He walked back to the counter.

Garry Reimer was a few minutes early. I recognized him immediately when he walked in the door. The E-Galaxy photo had shown a man with medium-brown hair, hazel eyes and a sturdy body. Huge smile with a lot of teeth. Not exactly good-looking, but attractive enough.

He came over immediately. If I wasn't mistaken, he was wearing the same sports jacket as he had been in the photo. His smile was even bigger than in the picture.

"Jennie," he said. "I'm Garry. How nice to meet you." He reached out his hand.

"Hi, Garry," I said, giving him mine in return. He gripped it firmly but not overly so. I was glad he didn't try to dominate me with a handshake.

"Can I get you a beverage?" he asked.

I pointed to mug in front of me. "Still full."

"I'll be back in a second then," he said.

I watched him walk up to the counter. He strode with confidence but didn't swagger. All good, I thought.

He chatted to Caitlin while waiting for his order and gave her a card of some sort. I couldn't hear their conversation over the whiz of the espresso machine.

I glanced around the coffee shop. Some of the usual regulars were there. The older couple who shared the newspaper. Two retired men at the window table, playing cards. A man and a woman, both dressed for business, were talking over an open laptop. Several high school kids had taken over the easy chairs at the back. The buzz of conversation was louder than usual.

Garry sat down across from me with his mug. He gave me his entire attention.

"Now let's talk about you," he said.

I felt myself flush. This man wanted to know all about me! None of my dates before had ever said that.

"Well, I work in a bank—"

"Just a minute," Garry said. "My phone just vibrated." He took the phone from his inside jacket pocket and punched a button. "Jason! How are you, my man? Got the paperwork? Yes…Yes…" He looked back at me. "Sorry, I have to take this," he whispered.

I nodded to signal my understanding.

"That's all they offered? Screw them."

I cringed. Why did people on cell phones have to talk so loud?

"Go back with a counteroffer," Garry said into the phone. "Five fifty-four, not a cent less. And be firm. Don't let them dick you around, Jase, you hear me? Call me when you hear back." He clicked off and put the phone on the table between us.

"Sorry about that. So. We were talking about you." He gave me the thousand-watt smile again.

I sat up straighter. "Oh. Well, I work in a bank—"

"So you already have a mortgage then," he interrupted.

I hesitated, taken aback. "Not right now. I'm renting."

"But as a bank employee, you get a terrific deal on mortgages surely." His blue eyes seemed determined to hypnotize me.

"It's just that my husband died, and I had to—"

"You shouldn't be renting, Jennie. It's Jennie, right? That's like throwing money away. I could find you a place you could afford—damn it. There's my phone again."

His hand swooped down to pick it up. "Yeah, Rick, what's up? The Anderson property? Blow me."

I cringed again. He seemed to be even louder this time. Everyone else in the coffee shop had stopped talking.

"Yeah? Tell them to fuck themselves. I'm not losing this deal. Just do what you have to do and don't be a jackass." He clicked off and turned back to me.

Big smile. "Sorry about that. Where were we?"

Dave appeared at my shoulder. "You forgot your donut," he said. A delicious-looking French cruller appeared on a plate in front of me.

Except I hadn't ordered a donut.

I looked up at him, questioning.

"Who's your friend?" he said, glaring at the other man.

Garry Reimer stood up. He had on his biggest smile (I'd seen plenty of them) and held out his hand.

"This is Garry," I said. "Garry, this is Dave. He owns this coffee shop." I said it proudly, for some reason.

"Do you own the property?" said Garry to Dave.

"Yes," said Dave. His voice sounded tired.

"Live above it?" said Garry.

"No, I have a house not far away," said Dave.

"Thinking of selling it?" said Garry. "Here, let me give you my card." He reached into his pocket and pulled out a glossy business card.

"Not thinking of selling it," said Dave in that weary voice.

"How about a cottage? This business looks like it's doing well. You could do with a lakeside cottage. Great investment."

Dave shook his head. Then he fixed his eyes on me, as if he had just made a big point. "See you later, Jennie."

I watched forlornly as he walked away.

Garry sat down.

"So, Jennie, what's your price range? How much do you make? We should be able to find you something. Oh, wait. Is that Harry Newscomb over there?" Garry was up on his feet again. He crossed the room before I could answer.

"Harry, my man! How's things? How's that lovely wife of yours?" I watched as Garry slapped the back of one man, introduced himself to the other and then pulled up a chair to sit at their table. The business cards came out.

On the table in front of me, Garry's cell phone buzzed.

I picked up my purse and walked out of the coffee shop.

I was nearly to my car before I heard: "Jennie?"

I turned, expecting Garry. But it wasn't Garry. It was Dave.

"Here, take this," he said. He handed me a business card. I recoiled.

"No, it's not his," said Dave. "It's one of mine from the coffee shop. My number is on there. If you ever need me, just call."

I thanked him, fighting back tears.

"When are you here again?" asked Dave.

"Tomorrow morning," I said, fumbling for the car keys in my purse. "I promised my son I'd bring him here. For a treat."

"Checking up on you, is he?"

"Oh, most likely," I said, smiling in spite of everything.

"See you tomorrow then," he said softly.

→ → →

My cell phone buzzed while I was driving home. I didn't look at it until after I parked.

Charming? Angela had texted.

RONALD, I texted back in caps.

EIGHT

That night after Ryan had gone to bed, I pulled out an old photo album. One from before Ryan was born.

Greg and I got married six months after we met. Far too soon, I would tell anyone now. But it had worked out for us. We had been happy for many years and content for several more.

Okay, maybe that was a slight exaggeration. It wasn't a storybook marriage. Greg hadn't been much of a listener. A lot of men aren't, I know. He watched a lot of football and hockey on television, whereas I like to read books. He wasn't much interested in discussing anything I read.

On the other hand, I'm pretty sure he had wished I was the sort of gal who was interested in sports.

In the beginning Greg wasn't sure he wanted kids. He certainly didn't want more than one. But when he saw Ryan for the first time, he fell in love. Greg had been a faithful husband and a good dad. Not exactly helpful with diapers, perhaps. That fell to me. But he had provided for his family and never complained about having to do so.

He was a good guy. Not a Disney prince. Certainly not Prince Charming. But I had loved him.

I flipped open the cover of the album. This is bad, I told myself. Don't go there.

Like some message from heaven, the phone rang. I picked it up.

"How are you, darling? I was thinking of you just now and had an overwhelming urge to call." It was Mom, of course.

I smiled. Are all mothers clairvoyant? "All fine here," I said. "When are you coming home?" Oh dear. Was that too obvious? Would she immediately conclude that I was feeling lonely and sad tonight?

"A little earlier than intended. I'm tired of Florida, to be frank. Miss you guys too much. We're packing up now. Dad plans to be on the road by Sunday. We'll have a leisurely trip back. He's planned three overnight stops to break up the driving. So we should be home by Wednesday."

Wednesday? That meant I had only another five days to meet Prince Charming!

"Wonderful!" I said, not entirely sure if it was or not. Well, it was in one way. I missed them. But this E-Galaxy experiment was going to be impossible to conduct with my parents looking over my shoulder.

"We'll be arriving late, I expect," said Mom. "Your dad will be very tired."

"I'll get in basic supplies for you," I said. "Bread, butter, milk, cream for coffee. That sort of thing."

"Thanks, dear. Love to Ryan. See you soon!"

I clicked off, feeling happy. How strange. Was it normal for a person to go from sad to happy with just one phone call?

I put the photo album away and went to bed.

➤ ➤ ➤

We arrived at the Original Coffeehouse at nine the next morning. Some might consider that early for a Saturday. It isn't early if you have a twelve-year-old boy with a bottomless well for a stomach. And donuts were on the menu.

Dave was his usual cheery self when we walked in. I liked the way he dressed, in black pants and a black golf shirt. Neat-looking but casual. I'd never seen him in anything else, so it must have been the uniform for this place.

I did the introductions. Dave put his hand out. I was pleased to see that Ryan didn't hesitate to shake it. Nice of Dave to treat Ryan like an equal.

"The usual?" Dave said to me.

"No. It's morning. I've only had my starter coffee. Give me a large dark roast, double cream, no sugar," I said.

He chuckled. "One large coffee coming right up. And for you, Ryan?"

"He'll have chocolate milk and a choco-late iced donut."

"Mom! I can order myself," said Ryan, clearly annoyed.

What was with Ryan? He avoided my eyes. Instead, he continued to look at Dave, who was looking back.

"Moms," said Dave, shaking his head.

"I *know*," said Ryan. "They always embarrass you."

"That's because they don't want you to grow up," said Dave.

"Tell me about it," said Ryan. He rolled his eyes.

I really wasn't needed for this conversation. So I grabbed a few napkins and sauntered over to my usual table.

Ryan followed me back after giving his order. (My version was incorrect, apparently.) He plunked down in the chair. It was weird seeing Ryan across the table from me. That's where my dates usually sat.

"This place is cool. They have Wi-Fi," said Ryan. His phone was out. I didn't try to enforce the "no phones at mealtime" rule because technically this wasn't a meal.

Dave brought our drinks and donuts to the table. I am always amazed at how some people can balance multiple drinks and plates. Not me. I'd be a one-person comedy act if I tried to pull that off.

"Are you always here?" I said to Dave.

He shook his head. "Not always. Not Tuesday nights, for instance. That's gaming night at the pub."

Ryan lifted his head away from the cell phone. "You're a gamer?"

Dave glanced at me, as if embarrassed. Then he turned to Ryan.

"Yeah. Have been since I was your age."

"What's your main?" said Ryan.

Dave hesitated.

"What does that mean?" I asked.

"Main name," said Dave. "The main name you play under. You can have alt names—alternative names—as well." Then he turned to Ryan. "Dragonbreath."

Now I knew why he had hesitated. I started to giggle, but it came out more like a snort. "Dragonbreath? Really?"

Dave looked sheepish. "I know. Sounds silly. But you have to remember, I've had that name a really long time. Since I was a kid."

"Dragonbreath?" I said it again. It was too funny.

Dave shrugged. "Yeah. I kill them with my breath. Don't even need fire. They just keel over."

"I used to have a great-uncle like that," I said. I wasn't joking. We'd all avoided Uncle Reggie. "He's dead now."

Dave chuckled. "Killed by his own breath?"

Another giggle escaped me. I looked over at Ryan to see how he was reacting to this.

"*You're Dragonbreath?*" Ryan said in a hushed voice.

Dave nodded.

"Really? No shit?"

"Hey! Don't use words like that," I scolded. Dave was a nice guy. I didn't want him getting a bad impression of us.

Ryan turned to me. Excitement glowed in his eyes. I had never seen him like this before. "Mom, this guy is epic! He's legendary."

I stared at him. Then I stared at Dave, who seemed embarrassed. "Been doing this a long time," he said to me. "You get known."

"Wait till I tell the guys at school about this," said Ryan. "Dragonbreath lives in our town. Knows my mom! They won't believe it." Already he was tapping wildly on his phone.

The doorbell dingled. "Gotta get back to the counter," Dave said. He left in a hurry. If I didn't know better, I would have thought he was anxious to get away.

"He's famous?" I said to Ryan.

"Mom, he's beyond famous. Every gamer knows about him. I told you. He's legendary."

Well, well. I'd had a lot of surprises this week. But this one topped them all.

➤ ➤ ➤

On the way home in the car, Ryan was quiet. He seemed to be brooding about something. Finally, he said, "Mom, is Dave married?"

So that was it. "Yes," I answered.

"Too bad," he muttered, just loud enough for me to hear.

NINE

I dropped Ryan off at a friend's house. Then I did the weekly grocery shopping. Crazy to shop on a Saturday when you are off work all week, but old habits die hard. All this had to be done before my date with Jeremy at four.

According to his E-Galaxy photo, Jeremy was tall, dark and good-looking. He had one kid from a previous marriage. His profile said he worked in the entertainment industry. I had no idea what that meant. So I phoned Angela.

"Probably means he's an out-of-work actor," said Angela.

I thought about that. Didn't actors want you to know they were actors though? Why hide it?

"Or maybe he works in a casino," she said. "As a croupier."

This was possible. We did have a new casino on the edge of town.

"Or wait. He could be a male stripper. Wouldn't that be a hoot!" Angela giggled like a teenager.

"No, it wouldn't," I said into the phone. Anything but that!

"Can you imagine introducing him to your parents?" She was still laughing when she rang off.

→　→　→

I got there early, as usual. I wore the same black skirt and pink top so I would be easy to find. At four o'clock precisely, a tall dark-haired man walked into the shop. He was well dressed, in designer black jeans and leather jacket. His eyes swept the room until he found me.

Wow—he was handsome, all right. The kind of guy you see in underwear ads on billboards.

Jeremy walked over to the table and sat down. His eyes swept over me, but he seemed preoccupied. I waited for him to introduce himself. When he didn't, I talked first.

"I'm Jennie," I said cheerfully.

"No," he said.

"What?" I was pretty sure I was Jennie.

He got up from the table. "This isn't going to work. You aren't my type. Sorry."

He walked swiftly to the door and out.

I sat at the table with my mouth hanging open.

One minute. This date had lasted less than one minute. I felt tears welling in my eyes.

It was ridiculous. Why was I crying? I didn't even know this man, and he had made me cry.

"Jennie?" Dave stood by the vacant chair. "Everything okay?"

"I'm a Ronald!" I blurted out. I wiped a tear away before it could trail down my cheek.

Dave sat down. "What does that mean?"

He sat quietly as I explained. I told him all about *The Paper Bag Princess*. Then I explained the Prince Charming–Prince Ronald thing I had going with Angela.

"I remember that book," he said. "Robert Munsch was brilliant. Remember *Mud Puddle*? That was my favorite."

I nodded. We sat in silence for a few moments. I wondered what he was thinking. Back to his own childhood?

"Jeremy said I wasn't his type," I said finally.

"Jeremy is an ass," said Dave. His voice was harsh.

I didn't disagree.

"Dave?" called Caitlin from behind the counter. "The supplier is here."

"Gotta go," Dave said to me. "Are you here tomorrow?"

I shook my head.

"See you on Monday," he said. My eyes followed him as he walked across the shop and through an open doorway at the back.

➤　➤　➤

I needed some girl talk. So on Sunday afternoon, Angela came over. She was, as usual, dressed in a gorgeous designer knock-off. Shades of cream and raspberry. She looked like an escapee from a posh country club.

"Hope you're in the mood for something sweet," she said. "I brought two cannoli." She presented me with a bakery box.

"Oooh! Ang, you are a lifesaver." I took the box from her.

She threw herself down on my comfy sofa. "You sounded down. Tell me about this last guy."

While I pulled out a plate, I told her about one-minute Jeremy.

"What a jerk," she said when I finished. "I wonder if he's a one-minute Jeremy in the other department."

"ANG!" I was shocked, but she had accomplished her goal. I was laughing now. "Well, we'll never find out." I plunked the plate containing our pastries down on the wooden coffee table. Then I took my place at the other end of the sofa.

"So tell me about the next guy you have lined up."

I watched a manicured hand reach forward to snatch a cannolo from the plate. Angela was slim, but she had a fierce sweet tooth. Good thing she was tall.

My tablet was on the coffee table. I clicked to the E-Galaxy site and brought up Peter's profile.

Angela stared at the photo. She stuffed the last of the cannolo into her mouth and munched quickly.

"Major cute," she said after licking her fingers. "He looks a little like Brad Pitt. Not as dreamy, of course. But he has that basic blond, all-American look."

"Blue eyes," I said. I'd never dated a guy with blue eyes before.

"Wonder if he's a Charming or a Ronald," she said.

I groaned while reaching forward for my cannolo. "I've met five Ronalds already! Frankly, I'd settle for a Frog Prince at this stage."

"Don't give up, Jen. You can't give up."

"I won't. After all, there's the book." I had to smile. Now I was talking about the book. I would have to write it after all.

"Strange," Angela said, leaning back into the sofa cushions. "But this is the best part of it all."

"What do you mean?"

"The anticipation. Seeing the guy's profile. Wondering what he'll be like in person. Trying to imagine a future together with a man who you only know on paper."

I thought about that. "The problem is, when you finally meet him, you're usually disappointed."

She sighed. "That's the trouble with reality. Our imaginations are so much better."

TEN

I had arranged to meet Peter on Monday at five.

This time, I took a great deal of care with my appearance. I had a good feeling about tonight and wanted to look my very best. So I nixed the black skirt and pink top. Instead, I pulled out the best dress in my closet.

I didn't have many. I'd bought this one a little over two years ago for a Caribbean cruise. I had never been to the Caribbean. Greg had booked the trip to celebrate my birthday and our anniversary.

We never went on the cruise. Greg died the month before.

I loved to look at this dress. It was in shades of green and blue, like panes of stained glass. It had a V-neck and three-quarter-length sleeves. The hem came to my knees. It was time I wore the thing.

I did my makeup carefully. I pulled on nylons, then slipped on the dress. It fit well.

Peter wasn't tall, I remembered from his profile. Maybe five eight. But then, I'm not tall either. I decided ballerina flats would be fine with the dress. It was a warm April day. I could carry a sweater for later.

Ryan had arranged to have dinner at a friend's house. They would drop him home at eight. This was good, as it meant I didn't have to worry about feeding him and keeping him busy for several hours. Ryan was old enough to stay on his own. He was very responsible. But he did get lonely.

So I drove to the Original Coffeehouse, singing along to the radio all the way.

My E-Galaxy date arrived the same time I did. He actually held the coffee-shop door open for me.

"You're Jennie, right?" he said. His voice was warm and friendly. "You look just like your profile photo."

I was delighted. Especially since Peter actually looked a lot like his photo. As Angela had said, he was major cute.

At the counter Peter asked me what I'd like. "I'll get this," he said. "You find us a table."

Wow. This was the first time an E-Galaxy date had actually paid for my coffee. Things were looking up.

I sat down and looked back at the counter. Caitlin was serving him. I didn't see Dave about.

Peter was wearing chino slacks and a blue golf shirt. He looked like a pro golfer who had just stepped off the course.

We started talking as soon as he returned with our coffees. It was so easy to talk to him. He asked about the television shows I watched and the books I read. We liked a lot of the same things.

He even seemed interested in my son. "Have you got a picture of Ryan?" he said at one point.

I reached into my purse and pulled out my wallet. I handed the photo across to him.

"Good-looking kid," Peter said, handing it back. "He looks like you."

What a nice guy, I thought.

Eventually we got around to what we did for a living.

"I'm in the import business," said Peter.

"That sounds interesting. What do you import?"

"Spices," said Peter. "It's a family business." There was a twinkle in his eye.

"But it's cool. I get to travel a lot." He gave me a big smile.

I was starting to fall for that smile.

"Look, it's nearly six o'clock. I don't want this date to end," he said. "Can I take you to dinner?"

I beamed.

"I know this little place down in Little Italy. We shouldn't have trouble getting in on a Monday night. I know the people. Do you like Italian?"

"Love it!" I said. "My grandmother was Italian."

"Great," he said. "I'll just use the men's room here, and then we'll be on our way." He smiled warmly. I watched him walk away.

This could be it, I thought. He could be the one. Such a nice guy. And, better yet, he truly seemed into me.

My cell phone went off. I looked down at it quickly.

Ronald? texted Angela.

Might be Charming, I texted back.

I put my cell phone in my purse and stood up to wait for Peter. When he came back into view, he pointed to the door. I joined him there.

Just before leaving, I looked back at the counter to wave bye to Dave. But he wasn't there. Probably working in the back, I decided.

It was still light out. Peter led me to a late-model Mustang.

"Wow," I said, admiring the shiny black good looks. "This is gorgeous."

He held the passenger door open for me. "Fast too. Not that you can use all the power it has on the roads around here."

We had agreed to take one car since I didn't know where the restaurant was. I wasn't so good with directions. That would be just my luck! Find the date of my dreams and then lose him. Really lose him, as in getting lost.

It was safer this way. Peter would drive me back to pick up my car at the coffee shop later.

We didn't talk much in the car because Peter had the radio playing loudly. A little too loudly, for my taste, but I didn't say so. He opened the car window and let the sound drift out to the rest of the world.

La Dolce Pizza was across town in a small commercial plaza.

"I know it doesn't look like much," said Peter, "but you won't believe the food." He pulled the Mustang into a spot close to the glass front door.

I hopped out of the car and followed Peter into the restaurant. The next hour went by in a whirl.

They had a lot more than pizza on the menu. Peter suggested I try the seafood with spinach linguine. I agreed with enthusiasm. It isn't often I get seafood. I gave my order to the nice young waiter and then sat back to enjoy the ambience.

The little bistro made me feel like I was actually in Italy. Our small table was covered in a cheery red-checkered tablecloth. Lovely travel posters covered the walls. They spoke of ancient Roman ruins and sun-drenched Mediterranean beaches, in a colorful riot of blues and sunny yellows. Best of all, the aroma of tomato sauce emanating from the kitchen was simply divine.

As Peter had expected, there were hardly any customers on a Monday night. It was almost like we had the place to ourselves. I sat back in contentment.

The sound system was playing a collection of Louis Prima songs. I knew them all. It made me feel happy, like I was back at my grandmother's.

An older man came over to our table with two wineglasses and a small ceramic pitcher.

"Peter! How good to see you again," said the cheerful fellow in the white apron. He looked about my parents' age, with thinning gray hair and an ample tummy.

"Mr. Bartolli! Let me introduce my date, Jennie. Jennie, Mr. Bartolli owns this restaurant. His talented wife runs the kitchen."

Mr. Bartolli chuckled. "She runs me as well." He made a little bow. "Now please take this wine. It's on the house."

Peter's smile was brilliant. "You always take such care of me," he said.

"One of my best customers. And how could I not bring wine when he brings me such a lovely lady to look at," Mr. Bartolli said to me. He winked. I could see the dear man was a terrible flirt. But in a harmless way that was all fun. I was pretty sure if

I had been standing, he would have pinched my bottom.

Mr. Bartolli poured the wine and then left us.

"Try yours," said Peter.

I did. "It's excellent," I said. Such a nice crisp white, with lots of grapey flavor. I'm sure that's not how the wine critics would put it. But I liked it very much.

A basket of bread arrived with the waiter. Peter took a piece immediately. I resisted. I could almost hear Angela lecturing me about having bread and pasta in the same meal.

Peter talked until our pasta came. He told me stories about the foreign places he had traveled to. Like Asia and the Middle East. It was fascinating. I'd never been outside of North America.

When our meals came, we stopped talking in order to eat. I was grateful, because it was hard enough to keep the yummy sauce from dripping on me. I needed my full concentration.

The pasta was delicious. Lightly scented with lemon and garlic, not overpowering. Luckily, they had removed the shells from the scampi. I didn't have to fight with them. I was determined to eat every last shrimp and scallop, even if I didn't finish all the linguine.

Peter finished his dish before I did mine. He refilled his wineglass. I signaled no with my hand when he tried to top up mine.

He continued with the travelog, this time focusing on Italy. Specifically, the cities of Rome and Naples.

"You should go there," he said. "Especially since you are part Italian."

I was still happily munching my meal. So I nodded my agreement. I would love to go to Italy. As soon as I got home, I would ask my fairy godmother to arrange it.

Obviously, Peter didn't have a problem with money. And it never occurred to him that I might. It was also becoming clear to me that he was doing most of the talking. But I smiled indulgently.

It was nice to be out with someone so good-looking. His blue eyes sparkled. I had a hard time keeping my eyes from his. And he seemed so happy, being here with me.

This is a dream date, I said to myself. All that was missing was the red rose and the violin player.

When you marry young, there isn't a lot of money. You don't usually have dates that involve dinner in nice places. Greg and I had lived on pizza and cola through our courtship.

I finally had a real date, like ones you saw in the movies!

"Dessert?" said Peter. "They make a mean tiramisu here."

I shook my head. "I couldn't." I touched my hand to my tummy.

Probably I could have. But my waistline wouldn't thank me for it the next day.

The bill came, and Peter picked it up immediately. When I offered to split it, he put up his hand like a stop sign and shook his head. "I asked you to dinner, Jennie. No way are you going to pay for any of this. You can make me dinner sometime instead."

I smiled in pleasure at this. Peter wanted to keep seeing me!

It almost made up for the fact that I couldn't find my wallet. I had fished for it in my purse when the bill came. No sign of the thing. Luckily, Peter was engaged with the waiter in using the credit-card machine. He didn't notice my hands fumbling to find something that wasn't there.

Where could it be? I felt the butterflies of panic starting. *When did I last use it?*

And then I remembered. I had taken it out at the coffee shop to show Peter the photo of Ryan.

Thank goodness Peter had insisted on paying for dinner. I didn't want him to know what a fool I was, losing important things. Calm down, I ordered myself. We were going back to the coffee shop for my car. It wasn't late. They would still be open. I could whip in there and look for it.

"All ready?" said Peter, looking pleased with himself.

We both rose from the table.

"I really enjoyed that," Peter said. "Good food. Great conversation. A nice quiet evening out." He opened the restaurant door for me.

"It was wonderful!" I agreed. "Thank you so much." I was so excited, I almost skipped to the car. I couldn't wait to tell Angela. Maybe I really had found Prince Charming.

Peter held the passenger door open for me. I sat down, and he closed it, just like a gentleman. Then he scooted around to his side, got in and closed the door.

I reached for my seat belt, and the night exploded.

ELEVEN

irens blazed. Tires screeched. Cars screamed in from all directions.

"Shit!" yelled Peter. He reached for the door handle and tried to get it open. A big hand grabbed the door frame and held it solid.

"Don't even think of it, Anders." A burly, middle-aged cop reached in and grabbed Peter's upper arm.

"GET OUT OF THE CAR," a big male voice boomed through a megaphone. "PUT YOUR HANDS UP ON THE ROOF."

"I'm clean! I'm clean!" shouted Peter. The first cop threw him against the Mustang. He hit with a thud that moved the whole vehicle.

"Yeah, we'll see about that." Another cop ran his hands down Peter's body. He wasn't gentle.

"Shit! I'm clean, man! I don't deal anymore."

"Like we haven't heard that before. Spread your legs."

My heart was beating like jungle drums. Prince Charming was an outlaw?

"Miss?" I looked to my right. A policeman was addressing me through the window. "Can you roll your window down all the way, please?"

I sat paralyzed. I tried to squeak, *Of course*, but my mouth wouldn't work.

Thud. The whole car shuddered. "Fuck!" Peter screamed.

I rolled down the window.

"What's your name, Miss?"

I gave it.

"Can I see your ID please?"

I reached into my purse and handed him my driver's license. Luckily, I kept it with my bank-teller ID in a zippered compartment of my purse. Long ago at the bank, I'd been told not to keep either in my wallet. *It's easy to lose a wallet*, they said. Too easy, I had discovered tonight.

"How well do you know Peter Anders?" said the cop.

"This is the first time I met him." I gulped. "It was an E-Galaxy first date."

"I'm not carrying!" yelled Peter from a distance. I turned my head. There were at least three police cars surrounding us. Lots of cops. One of them was shoving Peter's head down to get him into the backseat of a police cruiser.

A small crowd had gathered at the door of the restaurant. I recognized Mr. Bartolli and several of the servers. A cell phone flashed as it took a photo.

"You don't want to go out with him again, Miss. He's a bad lot." The passenger door opened. "We're going to confiscate this car. I have to take you down to the station."

I nodded like a bobblehead and stepped unsteadily out of the Mustang.

The police car holding my date was already pulling out of the parking lot. That was the last I ever saw of him.

→   →   →

Thirty minutes later, I had answered all their questions as best I could. I cried only once. They were very nice and handed me some tissues. They made me sign a piece of paper and asked for my phone number. Then they said I could go.

"You keep away from him," said the burly older cop. "Got a rap sheet as long as your arm. He's nothing but trouble."

"Sleazeball," said the other cop.

Relieved! I was so relieved. There were two ways to look at this, I reasoned. Yes, it was appalling luck that Prince Charming turned out to be a villain. Who would have believed it? He'd been so nice. He'd seemed...perfect.

But I'd had a lucky escape. What if Peter and I had started dating steadily? What if he'd met Ryan, and they'd really liked each other? What if Ryan had found a stash of drugs...

I had to stop there. At the very least, this was a good one for the book I was supposed to be writing.

I couldn't wait to get out of the police station. Once outside on the concrete porch, I stopped dead. I had no idea what to do, where to go or how to get there.

Night was closing in. I checked my cell phone for the time. Nine twenty. I looked down the front steps of the massive brick building and tried to think sensibly.

My car was at the coffee shop. Not only that, I'd lost my wallet. It might be at the coffee shop. But it might not. I had no money and no debit card on me. I could get a taxi to take me to the coffee shop. But what if my wallet wasn't there?

Angela! I still had my cell phone. I could phone Angela. She would come to get me.

I tried her three times. Angela wasn't picking up. I didn't want to phone home and alarm Ryan. What could he do anyway?

What to do, what to do?

The idea came suddenly. I reached into my purse and pulled out a business card. I quickly punched the numbers into my cell phone and waited.

"Hi, it's Jennie. I need a really big favor..." And then I explained.

TWELVE

I was waiting outside the police station when Dave pulled up in the coffee-shop van. I opened the passenger door and slid onto the seat.

"Here's your wallet," he said, handing it to me. "I found it on the floor beside your table."

Whew. I gave a sigh of relief. "Thank you so much, Dave. And thanks for coming here. You have no idea how much I appreciate this."

"Worst date ever?" he said.

I groaned. "Another one for the book."

He put the van in gear, and I proceeded to tell him about the whole mess.

When I was done, he was silent. I expected him to laugh like he usually did after hearing about my disaster dates.

But he didn't laugh, and he wasn't smiling.

At last he said, "Why do you keep going out with these losers, Jennie? Why not me?"

I think the earth stopped spinning around the sun for one moment.

"But you're married!" I said.

"No I'm not. Whatever gave you that idea?"

I was completely baffled. "Angela told me."

"Oh." He took his eyes off the road for a second to glance over at me. "Yeah, I might have told her that."

Huh?

"Once. A few years ago. Before she met Zack. She seemed sort of interested. So I told her I was married. It was easier that way."

We passed King Street and pulled onto Main. My brain felt like fuzz. It was still trying to process what I had just heard. Dave was single? He wasn't married?

"I would have asked you out ages ago, but you didn't seem interested in me that way," he said.

"That's because you were married!" I blurted. Already I could feel my face going red.

"Yeah. Makes sense. Except I'm not," he said. There was a long silence.

We passed the high school I had gone to. Then the community center. He slowed down for a red light.

"Well, this is awkward," I said finally.

"Yeah, isn't it," said Dave. "Let me think."

We waited. The light turned green. Dave continued along Main.

Had I ever been so embarrassed? Did he feel the same way too? I wanted to crawl under the car seat and just wail.

"It's okay," said Dave. "I just thought of a plan."

We pulled into the coffee-shop parking lot. He parked right against the building.

"Come on," said Dave. He vaulted out of the car like a guy on a mission.

When we got to the front door, he held it open for me. Then he followed me in.

"Sit." He pointed to my usual table. I did as told, in my usual chair facing the door.

"I'll be back in a minute," he said.

"But—"

"Trust me," he said with a crooked smile.

And then he left the coffee shop.

I continued to stare at the doorway, baffled.

Almost immediately my cell phone buzzed. I looked down at the incoming text from Angela.

Did you call me? it said.

Too late. Her reply had come too late. How could I even begin to explain what had happened tonight?

A little dingle signaled the coffee-shop door opening. I looked up. Dave walked in. He stood for a moment, gazing about the room as if he'd never been here before. Then he spotted me sitting alone at the table. He started to walk over.

A big friendly smile lit up his face. "Hi. I'm Dave." He slid into the chair opposite me. "You're even prettier than your photo."

I swear my heart skipped a beat. Then happiness began to pour into it. "I'm Jennie," I said, catching on.

"I read on your profile that you like cooking and going out for dinner to try new places," said the man across from me. "I hope that includes coffee. I own this little coffeehouse on Main…"

He stopped then and held out both his hands. I didn't hesitate. I took them in mine.

And his eyes twinkled.

AUTHOR'S NOTE

One of the bad dates in this book actually happened to me. Can you guess which one? See www.melodiecampbell.com to find out.

ACKNOWLEDGMENTS

I want to thank all the usual suspects who passionately support me as an author: Cathy Astolfo, Janet Bolin, Alison Bruce, Cheryl Freedman, Nancy O'Neill and Joan O'Callaghan.

Many thanks again to Ruth Linka and her wonderful team at Orca Books. Working with you is an honor and a pleasure.

And finally, I want to give special thanks to the students at the Hamilton Literacy Council who begged me to write a romantic comedy. This book is for you.

Billed as the "Queen of Comedy" by the *Toronto Sun* in 2014, **Melodie Campbell** achieved a personal best when *Library Digest* compared her to Janet Evanovich. Melodie got her start writing stand-up and has since been a banker, marketing director, college instructor, comedy writer and possibly the worst runway model ever.

Winner of nine awards, Melodie has been both a finalist for and a winner of the Derringer and Arthur Ellis awards for crime writing. She has over two hundred publications, including a hundred comedy credits, forty short stories and twelve novels. Her work has appeared in *Alfred Hitchcock Mystery Magazine*, *Star Magazine*, *Flash Fiction*, *Canadian Living*, *The Toronto Star*, *The Globe and Mail* and many more. Melodie lives in Oakville, Ontario. For more information, visit melodiecampbell.com.

Melodie Campbell has also written the Gina Gallo Mystery series, books that are really capers more than mysteries.

READ MELODIE CAMPBELL'S AWARD-WINNING *Gina Gallo* MYSTERY SERIES!

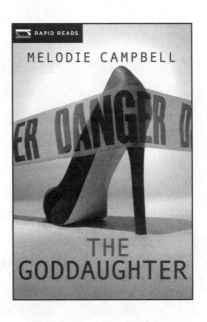

"Campbell tells a hilarious story of the goddaughter of a mafia leader drafted into a jewel-smuggling operation."

—*Ellery Queen Mystery Magazine*

"Campbell's comic caper is just right for Janet Evanovich fans. Wacky family connections and snappy dialog make it impossible not to laugh."

—*Library Journal*

RAPID READS
WWW.RAPID-READS.COM

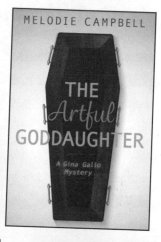

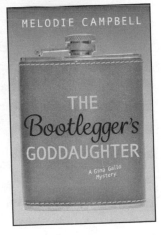

"The finest compact mystery series out there."
—*Canadian Mystery Reviews*

FROM BESTSELLING AUTHOR
Gail Anderson-Dargatz

Cookie is about to lose her job at the local bakery. She dreams of owning her own bakery but doesn't think she has the skills or money to do it. Most of all, she doesn't have the self-confidence. When she takes a course at the local college, she finds she has much more going for her than she imagined. With the help of her community, she figures out how to make sure no one has to go without her famous doily cookies for long!

"A master storyteller."
—*The Toronto Star*

RAPID READS
WWW.RAPID-READS.COM